AF445801

CHRISTMAS DELIGHT

NIGHT'S BLISS BOOK 2.5

E.C. LAND

CONTENTS

CHRISTMAS DELIGHT

This book is a work of fiction. The names, characters, places, and incidents are all products of the author's imagination and are not to be construed as real. Any resemblances to persons, organizations, events, or locales are entirely coincidental.

Christmas Delight. Copyright © 2022 by E.C. Land. All rights reserved. No part of this book may be used or reproduced in any manner whatsoever without written permission from the author, except in the case of brief quotations used in articles or reviews. For information, contact E.C. Land.

Cover Design by Clarise Tan, CT Cover Creations

Editing by Jackie Ziegler

Formatting by E.C. Land

Proofreading by Kim Lubbers

✻ Created with Vellum

TRIGGER WARNING

This content is intended for mature audiences only. It contains material that may be viewed as offensive to some readers, including graphic language, dangerous and sexual situations, murder, rape, and extreme violence.

Proceed with caution. This book does entail several scenes that may very well be a trigger to some.

Also, tissues are a must with other scenes.

Not for the faint at heart.

If you don't like violence and cannot handle certain subjects, then this is not a book you'll want to read.

CHAPTER ONE

Four months ago, my heart made itself known after years of only being used for pumping blood into my veins. My brothers and I have been working non-stop at taking out our father and uncles—forcing them out of their seats as head of the house. Danti ended up killing Preacher while I handled our father alongside our little brother, Benito. Emilio unfortunately went to ground and no one has heard a word about him.

Danti told Benito and me about our little sister and her being protected by Finley, the owner of Night's Bliss and someone with whom we made a deal to ally ourselves with. Arwen was being protected by Finley's right-hand man, Cedric. How the irony goes that Cedric is also the half-brother to the bastard who caused trouble for my sister in the first place.

But what has my heart beating once more is the woman I saw on the couch. The one I thought was dead. She went missing so many years ago, only for me to find out she's been alive all this time. For the past several days, I've been giving her and my sister time to heal after what they went through. I don't know for sure yet what exactly happened, but I know that it had to be hell for them. At least that's what I can tell from the bruises marring their bodies.

Done with waiting, I need to talk to Finley and Cedric and ask them about Mara-Lee. More than anything, I need to know what happened to her. She's not the same as she once was, but that doesn't mean I don't want her any less.

***

Checking the time on my Rolex, I step out of my BMW and walk to the back door of Night's Bliss, where I'm met by one of Finley's security team.

"Take the stairs to the third floor, they're waiting

for you," the guy says, jerking his chin to the stairs just as I enter.

Nodding, I take the stairs up and step into the office to find Cedric and he's talking to Finley while they wait on me to join them.

"Hello, Finley, Cedric," I say, offering my hand to both of them to shake.

"How's it going, Amer?" Finley asks, eyeing me curiously.

"You know, living the dream." I shrug, take a step back, and glance between the two of them. "I have a question about one of your employees."

"Who?" Finley asks.

"Mara-Lee."

Finley narrows her eyes at me. "What do you want to know about her? Does this have something to do with you calling her Stellina the other day?" She becomes protective.

"I know Mara-Lee and I want to make sure that she's doing okay." I'm not trying to give away my real reason for asking about her. Not yet.

"How do you know her?" Cedric asks, taking a step closer to me as his voice lowers, brows creasing.

"Stellina and I know each other from the past. I went to school with Mara-Lee's older brother, Mallik. He doesn't know about her yet, but he's my right-hand man. I've known her since she was six. Then she went missing after her sixteenth birthday."

Finley studies me for a moment, as if she is trying to make sure I'm not feeding her a load of shit. She must see that I'm not pulling anything with her and nods. "Mara-Lee's been through a hell of a lotta shit. It's not mine or Cedric's place to tell you her past. What she went through is for her to tell you when she's ready. Only then can you know what happened to her. What I can tell you is her past keeps her from reaching out to Mallik and why he doesn't know where she is. You want to know what's going on and why she's stayed away all these years, you take it up with her," she states.

I should have known that's what Finley would say. Still, I have to ask, "Why hasn't she told him that she's alive and doing well?"

"Mara-Lee thought it would be best that he didn't know . . . that no one knew. Again I won't tell you anymore," she replies.

Nodding, my mind goes to the conversation I had with Mallick a few weeks ago.

I sit down in a brown Italian leather high-back chair across from Mallik, a face I've seen a million times in my life, but today it's different.

"She's alive, you know," Mallik says as he runs his hands through his hair.

"You talking about Mara-Lee?" I knew he was. We have this same conversation several times a year . . . ever since she first went missing.

"You know who," he mutters, breathing out a sigh. "I saw her. I know I did. But I called out her name, and she didn't even look in my direction. Fuck, I looked like an idiot calling out to her only to have her ignore me."

"Are you sure it was her?"

"I know what my sister looks like."

"Yeah, but maybe it wasn't her." Even as the words slip past my lips, a bitter taste coats them. I've never believed my Stellina, my beautiful Mara-Lee was dead. She was out there, and I wasn't going to give up on looking for her. "Regardless, we won't give up on looking for her. I miss my Stellina just as much as you do. She was meant to be mine."

"You know if we ever find her, you have my blessing to be with Mara-Lee. I simply want my sister back in my life."

I bring myself to the present . . . that conversation was merely weeks before my brothers and I took our positions in the family. Now that I've found Mara-Lee, I need these two to trust me in order to get to Mara-Lee.

"If that's the case, I have something in store for my

Stellina." I clear my throat and shove my hands in my pockets.

"What are you thinking?" Cedric asks, quirking a brow.

"I'm planning on taking Mara-Lee away for Christmas . . . no matter whether she wants to go or not. She won't talk to me in public and avoids all conversation with me. I need to take her somewhere private where I can get her to open up to me." I think for a few moments and the perfect plan comes to mind. "We own a lodge and cabins in the mountains. I have a cabin that's only for family, and I can take her there. She'll be safe and it's very private."

"How will you get her there?" Finley questions me cocking her head to the side.

"I'm thinking Christmas Eve. I'll come to the Fort and all but kidnap her if I have to."

"She's not going to go with you willingly, I can tell you that now." Finley shakes her head as she smiles. "She won't be expecting you . . . she could be in her pajamas for all you know." She laughs.

"Doesn't matter. I'll give her until Christmas Eve, and then the gloves are coming off ." I shrug.

"What if this doesn't work like you are hoping it will?" Finley asks me.

"I'll bring her back home, but I have a feeling once

the walls she has built up around her fall down, it will go as planned." I smile. "I know a thing or two about my Stellina that I'm sure you all don't. It's just a matter of breaking through her defenses."

Finley and Cedric look at each other and nod. "Okay, Amer, we'll help with your plan. But if you hurt her, you're dead," Cedric states. I know that he wouldn't hesitate to put a bullet in my head. Same as I would do to him if he were to hurt my little sister, Arwen.

"I completely understand."

Leaving Night's Bliss, I pull my phone out of my pocket. I dial Danti's number and wait for him to answer. Normally at Christmas we try to do something as a family, well as much as we can. This year I'm changing those plans.

"Amer," Danti answers.

"Just want to let you know I'm making plans for one of the cabins for Christmas."

"You finally making a move?" he asks, knowing me all too well.

"I am. I need to get everything in order beforehand cause once I get her there, I'm barring the door from anyone until I know what happened to my woman, and I have her back where she's been meant to be all along."

CHAPTER TWO

I watch as Amer leaves my office and turn back to face Cedric with a knowing look.

"Well?" He cocks a brow and shoves his hands in his pockets.

"This will be best for Mara-Lee in healing the wounds that were ripped open after years of healing." I nod. When I first found Mara-Lee on the streets, I kept her from being raped, only to find out the true nightmare she's lived. Out of anyone else in my life besides Ainslee and our kids, she means something to me. Mara-Lee and Cedric are my family, and I'll do anything to protect them. Even when it's protecting them from themselves.

"I agree with you. She's been through a lot," Cedric agrees. "But are we doing the right thing?"

"Yeah, I think it is. Mara-Lee's been through hell and back. You saw the way he looked at her when he first saw her again. She's it for him, I feel it."

"I remember her telling us about her past," Cedric states, nodding in agreement. He knows what I know when it comes to Mara-Lee and what she's been through.

"I was locked in the little room, and when I heard the doorknob turn, I knew I had to kneel, or I would get the belt across my thighs. I wished I was dead so many nights because I had lost everything that was near and dear to me. Everything, even the guy I cared about so much. That was all taken away from me. Then to have it happen to me again. I can't . . . I don't understand life sometimes . . ." A tear falls on Mara-Lee's face as she breaks down in front of Cedric and me.

"Please don't tell anyone else. I can't . . . I don't want them to feel sorry for me or anything like that. I got through this. I just need a moment."

"Take all the time you need. We are here for you, Mara," I say as I pull her into a hug.

"Thank you." She smiles, and I hope we really do have her back.

"When Amer comes to whisk her away, she isn't going to be happy. I'm not going to stand in the way. I need to make sure that Vex knows what is going on, so she doesn't try to step in and try to stop him."

"Agreed, but I meant what I said. If Amer hurts her, I *will* kill him."

"I would expect no less. Though I'm confident it won't come to you killing him. If anyone is going to get hurt in this situation, it will be him. I hope he is able to break through the shell that she has created to show the world. Mara-Lee is a tough woman, and it's going to take someone special to get through to her. If Amer loves her the way I feel he does, then he has a fighting chance.

Cedric nods in agreement, and we go back to work. I hope I'm right about him because I'm not normally wrong about people.

CHAPTER THREE

MARA-LEE

CHRISTMAS EVE . . .

Sweat coats my goose-bumped skin. My body shakes uncontrollably as the nightmare I woke up from still wrecks my body . . . flashes from when Arwen and I were kidnapped. What they did to me, I'll never be able to forget—it haunts my dreams right alongside the ones that I thought were long gone. A tear escapes my closed eyes, running down the side of my nose, and I wipe it away with the back of my hand. I tell myself I'm okay and roll my neck to stretch my muscles. I look over at the alarm clock, and it reads seven a.m.

Dread lingers in my body, and I don't want to ruin anyone's Christmassy vibe, so I quickly get up and go to the kitchen. It's one of my favorite places to be. It makes me feel like I'm contributing to the family . . . plus, no one else is really worth a damn at the stove. Coffee has been made, so I grab a mug from the cabinet and pour myself some. Hearing the soft murmuring voices in the other room, I put up a front quickly to keep them from seeing how much I'm not myself today.

As much as I would love nothing more than to hide in my room all day, I'm going to try to hang and prolong the inevitable. Scenes from my nightmare flash in my mind, and I can't escape them. I want to run as far away from them as I can, but it's hard to run away from the past.

I go to my closet and pick out clothes that make me feel good and are comfortable. The shower won't take long to heat up. I get everything ready and turn on the water, allowing it to get warm and get in. I hope the water will wash away the mood I'm in and clear my mind. I want to be in a better mood since it's Christmas Eve.

After twenty minutes, my mood still hasn't

improved, and I just want to run as far away as I can so I'm not a burden to anyone. It's as if a sense of fear lingers over me, and I don't understand it. The lack of restful sleep is playing with my head, and I talk myself into getting back into bed after I get dressed.

I get into bed and pull the covers up around me, and I pray before I close my eyes to let the visions go away so I can rest. As I release a deep breath, I feel myself sinking into the bed, and peacefulness over-takes me.

A noise in the kitchen awakens me, and I know it's time for me to interact with someone, or they will figure out that something is wrong. I put my front into place so no one sees how I'm not okay, how I'm not myself. They don't need to carry the burden of this fuckedupidness I lived through.

"Morning, Mara-Lee," Finley says as she pours her coffee.

"Morning." I give her a smile, catching the knowing look in her gaze. When it comes to Finley, you can't hide much from her, no matter how much you try. I hesitate and fumble to get the milk from the fridge.

"I hope we didn't wake you up. The baby is in love with the lights and the tree." She smiles.

"No, not at all. I was already awake and ready for the day."

"I'm cooking breakfast. Do you want some? I'm making pancakes and eggs."

"No, thank you, not if you're cooking." I joke. "Why don't I cook them? We don't want the Fort to burn down."

"Ha, ha, ha, you think you're funny," Finley says, rolling her eyes. "Fine, we'll order from the diner down the road. That way, no one has to cook."

"That works for me." I didn't want to cook breakfast, at least not yet. I intended later on to fix the cookies, which I've already got ready for me to put on sheets in the fridge. But also, I'm not in the mood today, and I'm trying to pretend I am.

God, I wish I weren't, though. The nightmares have me shook to my very core, and I can't let them go. Finley has already gone into the other room, probably getting on the phone to order food for everyone. Knowing my time is limited, I duck into my bedroom before she comes back into the kitchen.

The feeling I have for not being around them makes me even more emotional, especially since it's Finley and Vex's baby's first Christmas, but I don't want to bring them down. This is a time for them to be happy and not ruined because I can't pull myself from what happened to me.

I lie back down and curl up in the middle of my bed after I grab the phone off the nightstand. I read through the messages I've received from everyone wishing me a Merry Christmas, hoping that I'm doing okay . . .

Unable to sleep, I decide it's time to stop hiding in my room. It's Christmas Eve and everyone here is my family. I don't want to ruin it. Especially for what Cedric has in store. He went all out with decorations this year . . . wanting to make it memorable for Arwen. God, the irony of how things turn out, but I'm truly happy for the both of them. They deserve all the happiness in the world.

Joining the festivities was definitely a good idea. For hours now, we've sat around watching Christmas movies. Cedric suggested we get hot cocoa. The guy has a sweet tooth unlike anything, though, he'll deny it anytime it's brought up.

Settling in for another movie and cocoa in hand and the fireplace roaring fire, I nearly jump out of my skin at the sound of someone banging on the front door.

"What the hell?" I snap, furrowing my brow, my

heart nearly beating out of my chest. Who would be here, banging on the door like that.

"I'll go see who it is," Cedric declares smoothly coming out of his seat.

"I'll go with you," Finley adds, joining Cedric and heading for the door.

Glancing between Vex and Arwen, we share a questioning look. But unlike them I know Finley and Cedric have to know who it is. They were far to calm when it comes to someone banging on the door. Especially today of all days.

A moment later, my heart nearly jumps from my chest as Amer, comes storming in, his eyes locking with mine. Its all I can do to swallow past the nerves threatening to choke me.

"Amer," Arwen calls his name, but he doesn't falter in his direction. His entire focus is on me.

Amer moves in, carefully takes my mug of cocoa, and sets it down on the coffee table.

I open my mouth to say something but he surprises me yet again by bending and lifting me in a fireman's hold.

"What are you doing?" I demand as I swallow my panic down.

"I'm done waiting for you to come to me."

Amer turns, ignores me kicking him, and speaks to

his little sister. "Merry Christmas, Arwen, I'll see you later." With that said, he starts walking again.

As he walks by I hear Vex asking Finley something and her responding with a snort and saying something about filling her in later.

"Put me down," I scream and hit his back as he carries me through the Fort and outside. The cooler air nips at my skin. What the fuck? Why didn't anyone stop him from taking me away? He places me in the car, not even looking at me as he shuts the door. I look at the entrance to the house and I realize they were all in on whatever Amer planned. Not a single one of them are demanding answers for what he's done.

I don't know who to be mad at the most right now, Amer or my so-called family.

CHAPTER FOUR

AMER

The drive into the mountains is beautiful, but not as beautiful as the woman next to me. I was hoping during this four-hour drive Mara-Lee and I would be reconnecting. Instead, she's given me the silent treatment. Only speaking when it's necessary. I'm not saying I don't deserve it, but I also don't mind. Everything is planned out and ready for when we get to the cabin. Mara-Lee deserves to be cherished and pampered, and I'm going to make sure that she knows how much I still care for her. I hope over the years that she has held on to the feelings she's had for me too.

I'll never forget her last birthday that we spent together. That birthday changed my life.

I look at the box sitting on my desk a thousand times. I've never been so nervous in my life. When I picked out this present for Mara-Lee, I thought of no one but her when I saw it. It's the perfect birthday present for her. We have plans to see each other in a bit.

My family's get-together is coming to an end, so I leave to meet with Mara-Lee. I get to her house and knock on the door, and it quickly opens. She looks breathtaking. I've always had a feeling that she was the one for me, but it's hard to tell your friend that you're in love with his younger sister. But I was.

"Amer." A smile unlike any other forms on her face as she holds the door open.

"Happy birthday, Stellina." I couldn't wait any longer to give her the present I picked out, and I hand her the small, wrapped box.

"Oh, thank you!" She smiles, then unwraps the box and removes the lid. "Amer, it's beautiful." She holds up the necklace; it has a cross with a heart in the middle, and centered in the heart is an obsidian stone.

"Do you like it?" I ask as I help her put it on.

"I love it. I'll never take it off."

"Good. I'm glad."

I pull her into my arms and kiss her quickly, because I

don't want us to get caught. Not yet. I know I have to do things the right way to get her hand in marriage.

"How was Christmas with your family?" I ask.

"It was good." She smiles, reaching up to touch the necklace.

"That's good, I know you all are probably still busy, so I'll let you get back to it, but I wanted to see you on your special day."

She kisses me on the cheek, and I leave.

A week later, Mara-Lee was gone. Leaving the necklace on her bed. That moment changed me as a person, and as I went along in life, I realized it changed me as a man. I was kind of naive about the world but losing Mara-Lee showed me what the world was going to be like. That anger and bitterness turned me into the man I am today.

Growing my wealth and power became important to me. Over the years, my brothers and I bought several acres of land. We decided that this land would be the perfect place for a resort and built ten spacious cabins and a magnificent lodge that sits in the middle. The property contains a heated pool, a tennis court, a couple of basketball courts, hiking trails, and each cabin has a hot tub. The cabin we're staying in is reserved for Danti, Benito and me to use. I've never brought anyone here before. Mara-Lee will be the first.

Losing her all those years ago made me see life differently, and I treated life in a different way than I would have if Mara-Lee had been beside me all these years. The businessman I am today came from me learning at a young age that life isn't fair, and if you want something, then you go after it and get it no matter what it takes. If you have to kill someone, then you kill them. And not with kindness.

Mara-Lee was supposed to be mine, and I want her back in my life. Once I found out that she was alive, I thought she would come to me, tell me what had happened, but she didn't. I tried to seek her out, but she put up wall after wall, so I gave her time. It's been long enough, and I'm tired of waiting for her. That's why I had to put this plan into action, with the blessing of her friends. I hope it works out for us.

After a stop to grab drinks and snacks, I don't stop again until I get to the cabin. I sent a text to my brother to make sure everything that needed to be finished last minute would be completed before we arrived.

As I turn onto the road to the lodge, I see the road has been plowed. Then I turn right onto the drive that takes us to the private cabin, and the snow has been removed all the way to the cabin. I park the car and move to Mara-Lee's side of the car and carry her inside.

I knew when I kidnapped her she wasn't going to be wearing any shoes or have a coat. It's why I made sure the cabin would be warm, and I bought her some clothes with the help of Finley telling me her size before going to the Fort. I open the large wooden door, and the warm air greets us. I walk through the door, closing it behind me.

The inside is warm and toasty, and a fire is burning in the living room fireplace. I carry her to the fireplace and place her down where she can warm herself.

"Are you going to talk to me or continue to give me the silent treatment?" I ask her as she rubs her hands in the heat of the fire.

She looks up at me, and if looks could kill, I would be dead.

CHAPTER FIVE

MARA-LEE

I close my eyes and allow myself to warm up next to the fire as anger pours into every molecule of my body. I can't believe Amer brought me to the middle of nowhere. I'm freaking out on the inside due to being surrounded by trees with no one around. Not a freaking soul. I didn't see another cabin around here when we pulled in. I'm trying to keep it all in. I keep rubbing my hands together to keep them from shaking. He doesn't need to know I'm scared because only Cedric and Finley know my past.

"While you're figuring out if you are going to talk

to me, I'm going to bring my bag inside the cabin. I got some things for you, and they're in the bedroom. I'll show you when I come back in." He turns and leaves, and I watch him walk out of the room, leaving me alone in the cabin.

My chest tightens, and I can't breathe. I stand to walk to the door to be close to Amer, but my legs give out from the lack of oxygen, and I crumple to the floor. I will myself to get up, but I'm unable to stand or see straight. I close my eyes and let the darkness take over.

"Fucking hell! Mara-Lee, what happened?" I barely hear him run over to me, and he places his hand on my face. My eyes flutter open, and I see the concern on his face, then he scoops me up gently and lays me on the couch. "Do you need a glass of water?"

I shake my head, and being in his presence calms me. My thoughts clear as my breathing evens out, and I take a deep breath and let it out, ready to go to battle with Amer.

I look up at him. "Why did you bring me here? Why the middle of nowhere? Couldn't you have just left me alone?"

"I brought you here because I wanted to talk to you since you continue to blow me off whenever I've tried to talk to you when I've seen you. I own this property with my brothers, so I know it's somewhere safe and no one will bother us. I couldn't leave you alone anymore. I was tired of waiting . . . I've waited for you for so long."

"You don't just take someone one because you want to talk to them, Amer. I can't believe you brought me here. What were you—" Amer stops the words coming from my mouth by kissing me as he wraps his arms around me. Zaps of electricity fly through my body and what I felt for him all those years ago threatens to surface.

I relax into his arms and let myself enjoy his lips on mine. His tongue teases my lips, wanting full access to my mouth. I deepen our kiss, giving him what he wants as he takes control. I'm letting him take control. He pulls out of the kiss, breathless.

"I want inside of your Mara-Lee. I've wanted you all these years, and now that you're here, I can't wait to pleasure you." He kisses that spot behind my ear, and I almost come undone.

Amer stands from the couch and removes his suit jacket and tie, then kicks off his shoes and socks. He slowly unbuttons his dress shirt, and I feel like I'm watching a strip tease as he takes his time sliding off his shirt. His tan, muscular chest has a sprinkling of black hair, but there's a trail that disappears under the waistband of his slacks. I look up at him and our eyes meet. He smirks as he knows what I am looking at. He unfastens his belt, then pops the button on his pants open. I bite my lip as he unzips his pants.

He stops and holds his hand out for me to take. I grasp it, and he pulls me into him, kissing me softly as he runs his hands down my body. He steps back, lifts my shirt over my head, hooks his thumbs in my yoga pants, and pulls them down. I hear him gasp as he sees I'm not wearing panties.

I stand before him in only my bra., I reach behind me and quickly unfasten it, letting it fall to the floor.

"You're fucking beautiful," he says as he wraps his hand in my hair behind my neck and roughly kisses me like it's the first time he's ever seen me. He releases me and pushes his slacks and boxers down, freeing his hard-on. My eyes widen as I see his size, and I don't know if I'll be able to handle him.

He must have noticed my panic. "Don't worry, Stellina, I'll fit." I haven't heard Stellina since I was sixteen, a lifetime ago.

Amer steps toward me and completely consumes my body, and I feel like I'm floating in air as he picks me up and lays me down on something soft in front of the fireplace. He sits himself between my legs, and I assume he's going to slam into me, ripping me to pieces, but he doesn't.

He begins to massage my feet and legs with feather-like touches, kissing every inch of my body as he goes. I relax and let my arms fall to my sides. My fingers caress the fur of the rug as my body completely relaxes as Amer touches every inch of me, ending with playing with my hair.

"I'm going to go slow, Stellina. Please let me know if I'm hurting you."

"I will." I tell myself that it will be fine, and I relax.

Amer buries his face in my hot center, dipping his tongue into my wetness, then sucks on my nub. I'm dripping wet as I feel the tip at my entrance, and he slowly thrusts in, slow and anticipating nearly pushing me over the edge.

"Please," I beg.

"Are you sure?"

"Yes," I breathe.

He thrusts fully inside of me, stilling as I adjust to his size, and he begins a rhythm of in and out that has been quickly climbing to my release. I wrap my legs around his waist and pull him close to me. Amer leans down and our lips meet. I wrap my arms around his neck and deepen our kiss as his speed increases and the sound of our bodies coming together echoes around us.

I moan in his mouth and gasp for air as I fall over the edge, and I feel myself come on Amer's cock as he continues to fill my core. He growls as I feel his body tense, He jerks as he comes inside of me, and I come again as thrusts of Amer finding his release sends jolts of pleasure through my body.

Holy shit. That was amazing. But what just happened?

CHAPTER SIX

AMER

$\mathcal{I}$ don't want to remove myself from inside of her, but if I don't, then I'll fuck her again and again, so I lie on the rug next to Mara-Lee in front of the fireplace. I feel guilty for what we just did, but I don't regret it. Being with her was better than I ever imagined, and the way our bodies fit together is like she was made for me. I close my eyes and breathe in, relaxing as I breathe out and take in every moment of me being with her.

I've wanted her for what seems like forever and thought I lost my chance when she'd been kidnapped, and no one could find her. Not that we didn't try. I spent so much time looking for her and I always came up empty. As the months turned into years, the leads went cold, and we all thought she was gone forever.

Honestly, I can't believe I'm here with her. It's like a dream that I've waited for so long to come true.

I clear my throat before I speak. "Why didn't you let me know that you were okay? Or where you were all these years?" I gently ask, trailing my fingers along her side. I don't want her to put up the walls she's let down.

"I was getting ready for a New Year's Eve party at the house, and I didn't have everything on that I wanted to wear," Mara-Lee whispers, barely louder than a breath. She rolls to face the fireplace. "I was putting on the necklace you got me when there was a knock at the front door. Mom yelled for me to answer it so I did. I didn't understand what was going on, but one thing led to another, and he took me away from my parents' house under the pretense that it was what my parents wanted me to do, but he lied. He took me to a house that was familiar and pretty, but once I got inside, it all changed. I became his slave, and he was my master.

"He did everything and anything he wanted to me . . . I had no say in what he did to me. I was used, abused, raped, assaulted . . . everything. I don't even know how long I was there because the day ran into night and nights ran into mornings. I was locked away in a room with a small bed with no windows, and I wasn't provided with much. Just enough food and water to stay alive." She begins to tremble. I sit up and pull her into my chest, wrapping her in my arms. As I lean back against the couch, I grab a throw off the back and wrap it around her.

"I decided that I was tired of being nothing, but a slave and I escaped. I didn't have anywhere to go and was living on the streets, trying to survive after being locked in a room for years. I was making some progress, I mean I was homeless, but that was better than being locked away in a room and being some-one's sexual object. One night, a guy was harassing me and wouldn't leave me alone. I couldn't fight him off and I was almost raped by him, but Finley and Cedric rescued me. They saved me from being treated badly again, and they made me feel safe. I went with them when they asked me if I wanted a safe place to sleep and to take a hot shower. Since that night, I've been with them." She licks her lips.

"I didn't want anyone to know where I was because I didn't want them to come and take me again . . . it's already happened and I was saved again, but I choose to not risk the man who took me away the first time to find me. I miss my brother, but until I know that person who hurt me all those years is dead, I can't take the risk of Mallik knowing I'm alive. I won't put him in harm's way."

Rage consumes me as I process what has happened to her. Never should she have gone through any of what she endured. Mara-Lee was always meant to be loved and cherished. By me, by her brother and those around her. The fact Mallik didn't know anything about this . . . about the way she was taken, surprises me. Someone went to great lengths to keep him from knowing. Whoever took her had to know who he was, who I was, and exactly who my beautiful woman was.

I push the thoughts of how she was taken to the back of my mind and focus on the person who took her away from me. The fucker that hurt her will pay. He will get what he deserves once I find out who he is. I try to control my emotions and take a cleansing breath before I speak.

"Who took you?" I demand, my voice barely better than a snarl. Fuck controlling my emotions. When it comes to this woman, I've over controlling shit. She needs to know the affect she has on me.

"No, I can't tell you." Mara-Lee rolls to her back, her gaze meeting mine and I see the fear in her eyes and I wonder if I might know the person.

"You know your brother is capable of taking care of himself."

"I heard . . ."

"So, you can tell me, Mara-Lee. You're not putting anyone in danger by doing so."

She shakes her head no. "I can't. I don't want to put myself in danger. If he finds out I'm alive, I have no idea what lengths he will go to ensure I'm dead. I'm sure he's powerful by now, and I can't. I won't risk my life." Tears streak down her cheeks.

"I hope one day that you trust me enough to tell me who hurt you. I promise you this, once I find out who harmed you, I will make sure they pay for ever laying a finger on you, then I will kill them. They took you away from me and your family and abused you. I'll make sure they never see the light of day again," I seethe, and I feel her tense beside me.

"I trust you . . . Life is looking up right now, and revenge isn't worth me losing what I have gained since then."

CHAPTER SEVEN

MARA-LEE

I debate in my head about telling Amer who kidnapped me, but I don't know his name other than it being Master. That was the only thing I was able to call him, because he was crazy. There are things I don't want to ever remember, but I remember his face, it's something I'll never forget. However, I knew his face before he kidnapped me too. That's why I went with him. I thought he was a family friend.

Talking about this is making me feel a way I don't understand, and I have all of this inner turmoil about what I'm feeling because it feels like I'm trying to come up with a reason I should feel sorry for myself.

I'm not that kind of person. I never went home because I felt degraded and unworthy of my family . . . of Amer. I wanted to find him so badly and let him know I was alive.

I wanted to go home to them all so much, but my pride wouldn't let me. I couldn't dare show my face after everything I went through. I was raised that my virginity was something that was important to give to my husband, and here I was a sex slave. I was trash in my eyes and thought it would be better if everyone thought I was dead.

When Finley found me, I'd been living on the streets and using sex as a way to get paid. I forgot what it was like to live after being locked in that room for years, and I had to do things I didn't want to think about to make sure that I had something to eat and some kind of shelter for the night. Life on the streets is hard, and I'll give people props for being able to make something of their lives after being out there.

The night Finley and Cedric rescued me . . . a guy almost raped me because I didn't want to give it up to him. He wasn't taking no for an answer. They saved me in so many ways and they gave me the feeling of safety, which was something I didn't have for a very long time.

From that point, I decided I wanted a new life for

myself and knew I could create it with them. So, I did. My life was great, and I viewed myself not as someone unworthy of being loved by her family but someone worthy of being loved because I was a survivor. However, the past has a way of coming back and biting you in the ass.

Even though I still had shit happen to me again, they rescued me and kept me somewhere safe. I have a good paying position at Night's Bliss, where I saw Amer for the first time in years. The butterflies I felt for him then are still there. He's a part of my past, but he isn't a bad part of my past.

The feelings I had for Amer have never gone away after all these years. I've tucked them deep down and kept them hidden for no one to see. Your first love is special and no amount of shit I've been through could take those feelings away from me. I've been with both men and women over the years. No one gives me butterflies the way Amer does.

"I do trust you . . . I guess I trust you with my life, Amer."

"You're going to tell me?"

I nod. "The guy looked familiar, like Mallik was friends with him or something. I'm not sure about that part because he really didn't say. He did say that he knew all about me and he was glad that he was going to be the one that got the first taste of me. The guy wasn't very old, but he definitely had some mental issues going on." I take a deep breath to calm my nerves. I don't want to remember the things the guy who took me said. The way he would talk about things he shouldn't have known. But then again considering who he was and the way he spoke so delusionally about things is mind boggling. I don't understand it myself. "He told me that if I ever told anyone about what I did to him, that he would kill everyone that I've ever loved in front of me and would kill me last. I believe he would. He's that mentally unstable." I shake my head shoving the memories of me chained to a bed, toys strapped to me and my hips bucking while he impaled himself on another toy.

"Do you think you could remember his face well enough to have a sketch done of it?"

"Absolutely." I would never forget the face of the man who tormented me for years in that room.

"In a week or so, we'll have that done." Amer reaches up to cup the side of my face, caressing my cheek with his thumb.

"Okay," I hesitantly respond, my breath catching.

Amer grasps my chin and raises it up, forcing me to look into his eyes. "I won't let anything else happen to you again, Stellina. You're mine, forever."

His lips slam into mine, and he isn't as gentle as he was earlier. He needs to claim me, making sure that I know, no matter what I've been through, I'm his. I roll Amer to his back, but our lips are still connected, and I straddle his thighs as I sit back down on his lap. I spread my legs, giving him full access to me. He releases my lips as he grins.

Amer grabs his cock, strokes it, and precum beads at the top. I lean down and lick the tip taking him in my mouth. I moan around him, lapping at the under-side, twirling my tongue around his girth.

"Fuck, Stellina," he hisses and pulls my mouth away from him. "Love the feel of that mouth of yours, but I need inside you. For too damn long, all I thought about was this. I need you again. I don't think I'll ever be able to go without sinking inside your pussy. So sweet and tight, and it's all mine."

He grabs my waist and lifts me up as he slides down a little, giving his cock and balls more room. Amer sits me back down, and I put my hands on his shoulders to balance myself as I position my entrance over his erection. He holds it as I slide down and moves his hand as I bottom out.

I allow myself to get used to the overly full feeling and I want to ride him like I would a pony, but he needs to be savored. Amer kisses me, and I don't want to move from this position, but I don't think that I can stay here forever. I use his body for leverage as I rise and lower myself on his cock, creating a slow burn that will have me orgasming over and over.

Amer will ruin me for all others and I won't complain. He says I'm his forever, but I don't know if forever is long enough.

CHAPTER EIGHT

AMER

I lie in bed awake and watch Mara-Lee sleep. She looks so peaceful as her chest softly rises and falls with each breath she takes. I'm taking in all of her features on her beautiful face and sexy body. In the morning light she looks like an angel, and I can't wait to claim her body once more. It's time for her to wake up.

Mara-Lee turns into my chest, and I take the opportunity to kiss her soft lips, then her jaw, and kiss behind her earlobe, planting kisses down her neck to the top of her chest. She softly moans and her eyes flutters open.

"Happy Birthday, Stellina, and Merry Christmas." I kiss her again and she wraps her arms around my neck as I pull her on top of me.

"Thank you. Merry Christmas to you too." She smiles.

"I think I can make it even more merry." I wink and tighten my hold on her as I rub my erection between our bodies.

I roll her over and slowly enter her wet center. Even after making love and fucking her last night, her body wants more of what I'm giving her. Mara-Lee is so responsive to all I do and quickly comes, as she screams out my name.

"I'm not stopping, Mara-Lee. I'll make sure that you remember this birthday." I continue to slam into her pussy and her nails dig into my back. "Yes, Stellina, grip me tighter."

My cock begs for release, but I deny myself, because I want to hear her scream out my name over and over as I ravish her sweet pussy for as long as I can hold out.

"Amer," she moans, and I feel her relax as she falls apart again.

I can't wait any more and I pound into her pussy as she meowls, wanting more and move.

"Fuck," I roar, coming inside, coating her walls

with my cum, not letting up until I can't move anymore.

I lean down and kiss her before pulling out of her and laying down next to her as I catch my breath.

"I'm going to shower and make us breakfast. You take your time getting up and showering, okay?" I tell her.

"Sounds good, thank you."

I pull her into me and kiss her again, then get out of bed to head to the bathroom. The shower is one of my favorite features of our cabins. I turn on the water and wait for it to warm while I brush my teeth, then I quickly shower.

Mara-Lee is asleep in bed when I step into the bedroom to get my clothes. I don't want to bother her right now, because I want to make sure my surprise has arrived. Once I'm dressed, I go into the living room. The Christmas tree that I'd requested to show up before Mara-Lee woke up has arrived. Everything is exactly how I wanted it to be. I get the presents I had bought out of the closet and finish decorating around the tree.

She's always loved seeing a tree and I want nothing more than to shower her with the affection she's deserved all these years. All the years that I missed out and this year I will be making up for all that lost time.

I head into the kitchen and open the fridge to the food I had delivered yesterday. There is a charcuterie board with breakfast meats, cheeses, fruits, breads, and spreads for us to enjoy while she opens her gifts. I start a pot of coffee and begin to head into the bedroom to wake up Mara-Lee, but my phone rings.

I look down at the screen, I see it's Danti so I answer.

"Merry Christmas, brother."

"I wish it was a Merry Christmas," he seethes.

"What's going on?"

"Emilio showed back up at the house asking where everyone was."

Anger courses through my veins. We haven't seen him in months. He disappeared after we took our places, having gone into hiding.

"Put him in a cell for the time being," I demand, not wanting to get into it over the phone.

"I've already done so." Danti isn't a fool like some might think him to be. He doesn't let anything get past him. The fact that Arwen and Benito both went through what they did isn't sitting well with either of us, but he feels the blame on his shoulders more as he's the oldest.

"Thank you," I breathe out, not wanting this to ruin my good mood.

"No need to thank me. He should have been smarter than to show here again."

"Agreed. We'll be home tomorrow." I refuse to ruin Mara-Lee's day.

"Okay, see you later." He ends the call.

Fuck Emilio. Why did he pick today of all days to decide to resurface? I push it out of my mind and focus on Mara-Lee. I need to wake her up so we can enjoy the rest of our morning together. We have plans later today, she just doesn't know it yet.

I walk into the bedroom and crawl into bed beside Mara-Lee. "Stellina, it's time to wake up. Santa Claus came and there are presents for you waiting under the tree."

She stirs awake and smiles. "Liar. There wasn't a Christmas tree here last night."

"True, but there is one here now, and there are presents with your name on them." I wink.

"Do I have time to shower before I go in there?"

"Yes, and all your clothes are in the dresser and hanging in the closet. I have coffee brewing so it will be ready when you come out."

"Thank you, Amer."

I lean down and kiss her, and she places her hand on the side of my cheek. Her touch zaps at my skin and I want her again, but I can't keep her in bed the entire time we're together. We need to connect in other ways too.

"If you need anything, call for me and I'll come to you."

"Okay." She smiles and I get out of bed to let her shower and get dressed.

I get everything out of the fridge and lay it out on the counter so it's ready for her to eat when she comes in here and grab two mugs from the cabinet for coffee. I pour myself some coffee and wait for Mara-Lee to come into the kitchen. While I wait, I try to decide how I'm going to handle my brother, and I feel like there isn't much I'm going to be able to do . . .

CHAPTER NINE

MARA-LEE

I look and smile, because I can't remember the last time I opened presents like I was a little kid and sat with wrapping paper surrounding me. Amer got me too much, and he told me it wasn't enough because of all the time we've lost. I had to admit it, but I'm glad he brought me here, because I'm in a better mood than what I was before we came here. Yes, I still have a lot of shit to work out, but he makes me feel safe. I know he won't let anything happen to me.

"So, what do you think?" he asks as he pulls me to my feet and into his chest.

I wrap my arms around his waist and lay my head on his chest.

"I love everything, but it's too much."

"Nothing will be too much when it comes to you, Stellina. Don't you worry about that. All I'm concerned about is if you like it."

"I do, yes. Thank you."

"You're welcome. Are you getting hungry?"

"A little."

"Good. We have reservations for dinner at a Chinese restaurant not far from here."

"That sounds good. Let me get my mess cleaned up and I'll get ready."

"No, leave it. I'll have the housekeeper take care of it."

"Are you sure?"

"Yes, go get ready, Stellina." He kisses my forehead and I release my hold on him.

I walk into the bedroom and look through the clothes that Amer bought for me, and I know they are expensive. There is a beautiful cream-colored sweater that is so soft with a small V and a black pair of pencil leg dress pants in the closet. I decide I'll wear them together with a pair of black booties, and I grab everything and lay it out on the bed, making sure it will go together. I head to the bathroom to freshen up and then get dressed.

As I walk into the living room, I hear Amer on the phone. I stop and begin to walk backward out of the room, but he motions me into the room.

"Sorry, I was calling housekeeping to come in while we're eating to take care of the trash."

"It's Christmas, Amer. I can clean up," I say as I begin to pick up the trash.

"Stellina, you'll do no such thing. We pay the staff well here and they won't mind getting paid to clean for less than an hour. They live on the property, so it's not that big of a deal."

"If you're sure they aren't missing time with their families . . ."

"Trust me, they will be happy to do it." He smiles. "You look beautiful by the way." He stands from sitting on the couch and walks over to me, then takes my hand and spins me around so he can see the whole look.

"Thank you. I'm ready whenever you are." I smile as I look up at him.

"Let me change my shirt, and I'll be ready." He winks and lets go of my hand.

As soon as he disappears, I move the trash in one pile to make it easy for housekeeping, and then I sit on the couch as I wait for him to change. I replay everything that has happened over the past twenty-four hours and I can't believe this is real. Maybe life is finally going to treat me well, and I'll gladly accept it.

I look up as I see Amer coming into the living room. He's holding a winter coat in his hands and I stand as he helps me put it on.

"Thank you."

"You're welcome. You'll need it considering how cold it is out there. A lot colder than what you're used to."

I zip it up and pull the hood over my head, not caring what I look like. I want to be warm. We walk outside, and he holds the door open for me. His car is running so it should be warm when we get inside. The path to the car is clear, and when I get to the vehicle, Amer opens the door for me and helps me inside. Warm air wraps around me and I'm so thankful for heated seats. I take my hood down and unzip my coat half-way.

Amer gets into the car and we drive away from the cabin. The snow shimmers in as the last of the day's sun shines through the trees. I feel like I'm in a snow globe as the wind stirs the powdery snow around us and I'm mesmerized by the way it floats in the air as we drive.

"This is light snow. The big fluffy snowflakes are better to watch. You can catch them on your tongue and have fun building snowmen."

"It's just so beautiful," I say as I glance at him and back out the window.

When he comes to a stop at the end of the main drive, he turns left instead of right. I panic a little as there's nothing but trees and snow all around us. A few minutes pass and a clearing comes as a village comes into view. Amer slows the car down and turns into a crowded parking lot.

"I'm glad I made reservations with the owner or we might not have been able to eat here," he says before getting out of the car. He walks around and opens the door for me. Then takes my hand in his after he closes the door.

We go into the very crowded building and walk up to the desk that's set up as the host station.

"Sir, there's a two hour wait," the woman tells Amer.

"I'm a personal friend of Jia's. I have a table reserved for two," he states.

She puts her lips together, as if she doesn't believe him, and she picks up the phone to call someone. "Just a moment please," she huffs.

Amer turns to me, "Sorry it's taking so long."

"It's okay. It's Christmas." I squeeze his hand gently.

"Amer!" a voice with a slight accent says from the other side of the station.

"Jia, it's good to see you."

"I'm glad you finally made it in. Sasha, take their coats." He looks at the rude woman and we hand her our coats. "This way, please."

The woman stares at us, unable to comprehend that Amer was telling the truth.

"So, how's business?" Amer asks as we follow Jia.

"It's going very well. Averaging an hour wait a night. It's unbelievable," he states, then stops by a door and opens it. "A private dining room for you and . . ."

"Jai, this is Mara-Lee. Mara-Lee, this is Jai. He owns this restaurant and comes to me for advice." He grins.

"Nice to meet you, Jai." I hold out my hand and he shakes it.

"Likewise. Let's get you seated and we will start with your first course." Amer holds the seat as I sit down, and he sits across from me.

"I hope you're hungry, Stellina, because you won't be able to stop eating . . . his food is amazing."

"I am." I smile and Amer grasps my hand and caresses the back of it with his thumb.

The food is served in courses and as soon as we're

almost finished with one another one comes out. I didn't think that it would take an hour and half to eat dinner, but it did. I'm stuffed, but it was a wonderful experience.

We get into the car, and Amer drives into the village, stopping in front of a dark building.

"Well, there goes that plan," he mumbles.

"What is it?"

"I wanted to take you dancing, but I guess they aren't open since it's Christmas," he states.

"That would have been fun."

"I have an idea then." He winks and drives away, and we head back toward the cabin.

Twenty minutes later, we are pulling back in front of our temporary home. Amer gets out and opens the door for me, offering me his hand.

"Be careful, it might be slick."

We make it to the front door without any issues and we get inside, where the living room is spotless and there is a fire burning in the fireplace.

"I'll take your coat," he says as he takes his off and I do the same, handing it to him.

I sit in front of the fireplace, warm my hands and think about how I could get used to sitting here all the time. Soft music floating through the room pulls me from my thoughts, and Amer comes back into the room with his shirt unbuttoned and his sleeves rolled up. He's sexier than sin, and I don't know why it's taken me this long to realize that.

"May I have this dance?" he asks as he holds out his left hand.

"Yes," I say as I place my hand in his and stand.

He places his right hand around my waist and controls us with his left. We dance for hours, and I don't want to stop.

"Stellina, I could dance with you anytime." Amer kisses me. "Let's change our clothes and get into the hot tub to relax our muscles."

"Is it outside?"

"Yes, the view is magnificent," he states as he guides me to the bedroom. "There are a few swimsuits in the dresser because I didn't know what kind you would like."

"Thank you for doing all of this."

"Anything for you," he says as he gets a pair of swim trunks out of another dresser. He walks into the bathroom and clothes the door.

I hurry and look through what I have to choose from. I find a cute black two-piece with crisscrossing strings. I walk into the closet and change, and I'm thankful I keep my lady bits neat and trimmed. There is a mirror in the closet, and I make sure that I look okay before stepping outside.

"Fuck, Stellina. That suit was meant for you." Amer stalks over to me and pulls me into his chest, kissing me and caressing my uncovered skin. "So, so beautiful." He kisses my nose, and I giggle like a schoolgirl. We walk through the cabin to the sliding door. "You'll need to put a pair of sandals on, and there is a robe for you to wrap up in too. It will be chilly getting in and out, but while we are in there, it will be worth it."

"I've never done anything like this."

"You will love it."

I bundle up in the robe and put the sandals on. He grabs a few towels, opens the sliding door, and I follow him outside. The hot tub is lit up, with multi-colors changing in the water and string lights hanging above the tub, softly lighting the path and steps into the hot tub.

There is an area right beside the steps that has hooks, and we hang our robes and take off our sandals. Amer ushers me to get in, and he follows behind me. The warm water feels good on my tired body, and if I could, I'd sleep here.

"What do you think?" Amer asks as he sits down next to me.

"This is amazing." I smile.

Amer stands and leans over the edge of the tub as he presses a button on a panel. Music softly plays in the hot tub, and I relax back into the seat.

Snow starts to fall while we're enjoying just being together. Amer pulls me into his lap, and I'm straddling him as he kisses me.

"The snowflakes in your hair make you look like an angel." He grins, and I notice something floating at the top of the water . . . my bikini bottoms.

"A fallen angel, right?"

"No, you will always be an angel to me, an angel who likes to do naughty things." He grabs my hips and aligns my center with his hard cock and thrusts into my core.

I moan out as he fucks me as hard as he can in the water, which isn't hard enough. He stands, holding onto me, and the cold air nips at my skin.

"Lean over the edge and spread your legs," he says as he situates himself behind me.

I do as he says and hold on to the side of the hot tub for leverage. He enters me from behind, and I find my release quickly as my vision spots, and I have to force myself to hold onto the edge. I don't want him to stop, I want him for as long as I can have him.

CHAPTER TEN

AMER

The past thirty-six hours with Mara-Lee have been amazing, but I know I need to get her back to the people she calls family. They mean a lot to her, and with Finley's baby just born, she'll want to spend some time with them too.

I lay here as the sun begins to shine in the bedroom, and I hold her as long as I can before we have to get up. Mara-Lee will be in my life when we get back, but I don't want to pressure her into moving in with me, although sooner than later, she will be with me.

"Good morning," she says as she caresses my face.

"Hey, good morning to you. How did you sleep?"

"Wonderfully. The hot tub relaxed every muscle in my body," she says as she stretches.

"Glad to hear that. We probably should get going, because the drive is about four hours."

"Just a few more minutes of cuddling?"

"Sounds good to me."

A few hours later, we leave the cabin to go home. While Mara-Lee spends time with those she lives with, I'll go spend time with my sister.

"Are you still angry with me for taking you away for Christmas?" I ask as we get back into the car at the last stop before I have her home.

"No, I'm not. This time away from the Fort has allowed me to let go of what happened to me. I know I have a long way to go before I'm healed, but I'm not in the headspace I was when you brought me to the cabin."

"I was hoping that you would say that because I enjoyed spending every moment with you, Mara-Lee. I hope you realize that I want you in my life . . . not just the past couple of days."

"You keep saying that . . ."

"I mean it. I want everything with you."

She's quiet for a moment as she thinks about what

I said, and she licks her lips. "I want that with you too." She looks at me with tears in her eyes.

"Oh, Stellina, I didn't mean to make you cry." I grab a handkerchief from my pocket and hand it to her.

"They're happy tears, Amer. I never thought that we would be here, together."

I caress her face with my hand, touching her soft skin, comforting her. She leans into my hand.

"And we will be together from here on out. We just have to figure out everything along the way. I'm not going to rush you into anything. When you're ready, we will move on to the next step. I'm not going anywhere."

She smiles, and I place my hand on her thigh and rub her leg through her jeans. Now that we are on the same page with where we are going in this relationship, I start the car and get us back on the road.

The conversation flows and I'm glad that Mara-Lee continues to relax and enjoy herself.

Nearly home, and my phone rings. It's Danti. Chills race down my spine as I know this call can't be good news. He knows I'm on my way back to town. Instead of putting it on speaker, I put the phone up to my ear and answer his call.

"Yes?" I answer with apprehension in my voice.

"You need to come home now, as fast as you can."

"What happened?"

"It's Emilio. He went off the deep end and killed Mother."

"What the fuck!" I roar. "I told you to put him in a cell."

"We did. Bastard somehow got out." Danti snarls.

"Fuck!"

"I called the doctor, and he is taking care of Mother's body. The cleaner is coming to take care of everything else."

"Where is he now?"

"He's tied up in a cell, but I need you here now, Amer."

"Fine. I'm on my way." I end the call and stop myself from throwing my phone as I see the look of horror on Mara-Lee's face.

"I take it that the phone call wasn't good news?" she murmurs.

"No, it wasn't. I have to go to my house."

"I can't. Please take me to the Fort before you go. Please, please," she begs as panic sets in her voice.

"I can't. I have to get there and handle something now. They can't wait."

"Amer, I don't beg, but I'm begging you, please take me home. I can't be there. Please," she begs again, and tears well in her eyes.

"Stellina, remember what I told you? I would not let anyone hurt you ever again. That includes my family. Do you understand me?"

"Yes, but—" I cut her off.

"There're no buts. You are mine, and I'll protect what is mine until the day I die, Stellina," I firmly state.

She looks down at the floorboard, knowing I'm not going to change my mind. I place my hand back on her thigh, soothing her the best way I can right now as I drive. Mara-Lee places her hand on top of mine, caressing my knuckles as I rub her thigh. She might not be talking to me, but this small gesture tells me she trusts me and knows I'll keep her safe.

I focus on the road and try to keep my rage in check. When I turn the car off at home, I don't know how I'm going to react. I need to keep my shit together so I know that Mara-Lee is safe. She is my main priority now, but this family business needs to be handled to assure Mara-Lee will be safe in the future.

I press the accelerator down a little more and pick up speed. The sooner I arrive at the house, the sooner all of this will be over, and I can move on with Mara-Lee at my side.

CHAPTER ELEVEN

*A*fter the phone call, Amer continued to keep me calm, ensuring me that he would make sure I'm safe. No amount of reassurance will calm me down. I'm freaking out as he pulls in front of the house.

"Stellina, look at me," he commands, reaching up to grip my chin between two fingers. I meet his gaze seeing the sincere determination in the depths of them. "I promise you, I'll keep you safe. Make sure you don't leave my side."

All I can do is nod.

He gets out of the car and walks around as a man opens my car door.

"Are my brothers inside?" Amer demands.

"Yes, sir. They're both waiting for you."

Amer grabs my hand and leads me inside. My heart's racing when we step into the house. I don't know what's going on, but I know something is not right, and I feel it as we walk through the house. I haven't stepped into the house since before my kidnapper took me. I look around as quickly as I can, and the place has changed so much. Maybe because Amer lives here now? I'm not sure, and now isn't the time to ask.

We walk down a hallway, and Amer stops, opening the second door on the left. Voices echo through the room, and I hear a familiar voice. When he comes into view, I freeze. I don't know if I should look at him or look away. I look at him, sitting in a chair with his arms chained behind his back, with Danti and Benito standing over him.

I try to hide behind Amer, but it's too late. Master sees me and starts cackling, a heated look filling his gaze. Unable to stop myself from doing something I've done far too many times and hate myself for, I fall to my knees, knowing that I'll probably not make it out of here alive. I want to run and never look back, but my body doesn't want to respond to any commands. My vision spots as I feel lightheaded. How can he be here?

"Stellina?" Amer kneels and helps me back to my feet. "Mara-Lee?"

I look up at him for only a split second before murmuring for only him to hear, "Master." I don't have to see his eyes to know he understands what I've just told him. His body tenses, and he wraps an arm firmly around my waist.

"Ah, Mara-Lee. How have you been?" Master grins.

I refuse to answer him or give him the satisfaction of me acknowledging him.

"Tsk, tsk, slave. That's no way to address your master now, is it? I'm sure you haven't forgotten how I ravished your body and toyed with you for so long. All the nights I brought you pleasure and pain. Can't forget about the pain. It's such an important part of our relationship."

Bile rises in my throat, causing me to gag, but I'm able to maintain my composure as Amer holds me close to his body. Flashes of what Master did to me play before my eyes, and I don't want to live through this again. I prayed that I would never see him again, and thought I would be safe here with Amer. But my rapist is in his house, still living and breathing. I thought Amer would take care of him . . .

"Oh, did you not tell my naïve nephew that I was the one that kidnapped you from your home the week after your sixteenth birthday?" He looks at me, then Amer. "Keeping secrets from me isn't a good idea, slave. I hope he punishes you." He laughs, and it causes my knees to weaken, and Amer pulls me back into his side, holding me by the waist.

"That's enough, Emilio," Amer grits out.

"You don't like that I fucked your whore first?" He smirks. "Just think every time you fuck her now, you'll remember I was there first." He taunts Amer, wanting him to come after him.

"You're fucking delusional. What did you do to our mother?" Amer seethes.

"I put that bitch out of her misery. She's old and didn't know how to shut the fuck up."

"What the fuck, Emilio?"

"She knew it was me who kidnapped Mara-Lee. It doesn't matter the amount of drugs in her system, she knew the truth, and without your father, me, and Preacher to keep her under control, she would have told. Stupid bitch, she was good for only riding a cock and her money. She begged me not to take Mara-Lee, though. But I kidnapped her because I wanted someone who was submissive and that I could easily break. When you kept talking about her, I knew she would be the perfect pet. She was too. At first, she was difficult. I didn't know if I was going to be able to train her, but one day she decided that she was going to follow my instructions. It was glorious."

"You raped . . . and abused her for years. How the fuck can you be proud of what you did to her?"

"She enjoyed it, didn't you, Mara-Lee? She got railed more than a ten-dollar hooker, and she was always wet and ready for me."

"You son-of-a-bitch. You're a fucking liar!" I scream.

Amer holds me and leans down. "He's not worth your breath. I'm letting him confess to my brothers what all he has done . . ." he whispers, then wipes away my tears.

"Oh, did I upset the slave? Too fucking bad. Amer, once I broke her, she was easier to train. She knows what down means, and the way she sucks cock . . . mmm. Probably could suck the chrome off a bumper with those lips." He licks his lips and winks as he stares at me.

I look away and glance at Danti and Benito. They look at each other in horror, not realizing what their uncle was capable of doing. I'm sure they knew but didn't put it all together until today. If I make it through this day alive, I'll be lucky, and I feel Amer's arms wrap around me, trying to comfort and shield me from his uncle's words. Amer's body tenses, and I know he is close to losing control.

"Amer, make sure she tells you whose name she was screaming out when I was fucking her tight pussy . . . yeah, she was screaming out for me, her master. She wanted me, and she probably still wants me, since I'm the only one who can pleasure her. I know every inch of her body. Isn't that right, slave. Who is your master?" He cackles, and goosebumps rise all over my body.

Amer lets go of me . . . and everything moves in slow motion.

CHAPTER TWELVE

AMER

All I see is red, and before I know what's happened, bones cracking greet my ears, and Emilio's lifeless body slumps forward in the chair. I had heard enough of what he had to say about Mara-Lee. He's lucky I chose to break his neck, killing him instantly, instead of what I wanted to do to him. Emilio should have suffered for what he had done to Mara-Lee and her family and what he did to me. I can't believe that my own uncle betrayed me like he did. At this point, I disown him. Fuck him. I hope hell isn't kind to him because he deserves everything that happens to him.

"What the fuck, Amer! Why did you kill him without explaining to us what you were thinking?" Danti asks as he tries to figure out what just happened. He stands there, looking at Emilio's lifeless body, then up to me.

"It's my right to have killed him for what he did to Mara-Lee and for betraying family. She was my woman years ago, and for the fact he took her away from me, I should bring him back from the dead and kill him again, repeatedly," I seethe. I look around and see Mara-Lee frozen in place. "Call the doctor and let him know that he has another body to take care of. At least this time, it wasn't messy," I command them.

"I will," Benito states, his lip curling in disgust as he stares at Emilio and pulls his phone out of his pocket.

"We aren't finished with this in the least, but we've had enough bullshit for one day." I rub my temples to ward off the headache that is brewing.

"I agree," Danti states. "We will meet here tomorrow at ten to plan the funerals. Mother at least deserves one even though she wasn't a mom in the least bit. Emilio can rot in hell, but we will decide everything tomorrow."

I nod and turn to walk toward Mara-Lee. She needs to get the fuck out of this room. I put my arm around her shoulder and walk her out of the room. I take her straight into my room, closing the door behind us for privacy.

"Stellina, talk to me," I say as I try to comfort her by cupping her face with my hand.

"It's over?" She looks at me, shock trying to control her body.

"Yes, I told you I would kill anyone who has hurt you . . . even my own family."

"Do you believe what he told you . . . the parts about me—"

"No, I don't believe any of that. He took advantage of you and he paid the price."

"Thank you."

"No . . . don't thank me. I need to thank you for trusting me that I would keep you safe."

I hold her in my arms as she cries. As her body trembles, I wish there was more I could do to comfort her. I hold her close to my chest and rub her back. After a while, she calms down, and her tears dry up.

"Will you take me home, please?"

"Yeah, I will. You need to be around all those people who love and care for you."

"Thank you." She attempts to smile but it falls flat.

At the Fort, Mara-Lee went straight to her room, not wanting to discuss what had happened yet. Thankfully everyone gave her the space she needed for the time being, but I could tell they were worried about her. Mara-Lee told me that only Finley and Cedric know about what happened to her in the past, and she will tell them how that chapter of her life is closed for good with Emilio's death.

Finally, after Mara-Lee showers and changes once again, does she let me pull her out of the room so she can be with the rest of those who love her.

"Mara-Lee! Welcome back. Did you have fun? How was your Christmas?" Finley asks. We step into the room I found Mara-Lee in that first time and again Christmas Eve.

"I did, thank you." She grins, and this time it's genuine.

"Good, you deserve happiness, Mara-Lee," Finley states, taking in the embrace I have around Mara-Lee.

She smiles and nods as she realizes that she truly does, no matter what has happened to her in the past.

We sit down on the couch in the living room. I don't leave her side, and she doesn't leave mine. I'm hoping that I can spend the night with her . . . I'm not about to ask her to come back to my place. As much as I love my place, I realize that I'm going to have to find another house to live in if I want Mara-Lee to live with me. She'll never be able to forget what she saw today. I wish I could. I force myself to focus on the now, focus on Mara-Lee.

I stay with her and see how she relaxes with her family as they talk and spend time catching up on what went on while she was away. This is her family, even though they aren't blood relatives, they treat her as such, and they saved her. They saved her when I couldn't. They've been here for her when I didn't even know she was alive. Now, she has all these people in her life that love her and care for her.

Mara-Lee might be mad at me once again, but I'm going to work on a plan to reunite her with her brother. Even though she already has a lot of people in her life, a big brother is someone that you need in your corner sometimes. Eventually, she should have everyone where they belong in her life again.

Losing Mara-Lee taught me that life can't always be full of bright, sunny days, but this year has shown me that a lot can change in a blink of an eye. I hope this upswing continues into the new year. An idea comes to mind.

I know how I'm going to get Mallik back into Mara-Lee's life.

EPILOGUE

MARA-LEE

I'm so excited for tonight. There's a party at Night's Bliss and Amer is going with me. Ringing in the new year with my favorite people sounds like a great start to the new year. I've been helping to make sure that everything is taken care of for the big party. The club is decorated, and there is plenty of food and drinks for everyone that is going to be there.

I get ready to head back to the Fort to get ready for the party. Amer will be picking me up, and after the party, we're spending the night at a hotel to make sure we bring in the new year the right way.

I stop by Finley's office before I leave the club.

"Hey, I'm headed to the Fort. Need anything?"

"I don't right now, thank you. I wanted to let you know an agreement has been struck between Danti and me," she states.

"I'm glad that it is finally taken care of."

"Me too. Now maybe I can enjoy my new year." She smirks, leaning back in her seat.

"Hopefully. I'll be back later. Call if you need anything."

"I will." She waves bye.

I head out to my car and drive to the Fort, and it's a little crazy. Everyone is getting ready for the party. I stop in the kitchen and get a snack before I head to my room. My dress is hanging up and ready for me to slip into. Amer hasn't seen it yet, and I can't wait for him to see me in it. I hope that he doesn't throw me over his shoulder and carry me out of here again. Although, that's hot.

He's sexy and mine. I'm thankful that he took a chance on me. I smile as I think about everything that has happened in the week that he has been back in my life. I have a better sense of balance and I'm healing.

I get in the shower and make sure I'm all washed and shaved before getting out. I quickly dry off so I can get to doing my hair. I'm going for a simple chignon at the base of my neck so that way my dress can show off every curve of my body.

My phone rings, and I answer it.

"Stellina, I'm on my way. Are you almost ready?" Amer asks.

"I am. I just have to put my dress on and I'll be ready."

"I'll be there in five minutes."

"See you soon." He hangs up, and I begin to panic.

I hurry and put my heels on, then put my dress over my head, trying not to mess up my hair and makeup. The zipper isn't too bad, and I'm able to zip it up the back.

I finish as there's a knock on my door, and I open it up. My jaw hits the floor.

"I don't know if I can let you go out in public like that tonight, sir."

"Why is that?" He smirks.

"Because every woman in the place will be trying to get with you. You better not get any numbers." I try to scowl but fail.

"No worries. I only have eyes for you in that smoking hot dress you're wearing."

"You like it?"

"Yes, I do. I can only think of one other place I might like that dress even better."

"Where's that?" I look at him confused.

"On the floor. . ." He grins.

It takes me a moment to get it.

"You have jokes tonight." I laugh as he pulls me into his lips, kissing me.

"Are you ready?"

"Yes, let me grab my purse."

We head out to the club, and soon, everything is in full swing. This year, I'm able to relax and have a good time. Amer doesn't go far from me, and every time I look over at him, our eyes meet, and the butterflies flutter in my stomach. No matter how many times I look at him, he makes me feel like a teenager again.

I'm lost in thought when I feel a tap on my shoulder, and I turn around to see who's behind me. Shock and surprise take over my body.

"I'm so sorry, Mara-Lee," Mallik says as he pulls me into his arms for a hug. "I'm sorry for everything. Please forgive me."

My gut clinches. I've missed Mallik so much. Tears run down my cheeks as he holds me in his arms. I don't know what to say. There's so much to talk about. All I can do is nod because if I open my mouth, I'm going to sob.

I can't believe I'm standing here with my brother, and I feel Amer come to us.

"Stellina, are you okay?" he asks as I stand back from my brother. He planned this. I know he did.

"I don't know if I want to be mad at you or be thankful," I tell him.

"Give it a few days and then you can decide." He smiles.

"We will catch up, Mallik," I tell him. "But right now, I'm going to dance with Amer."

I offer him my hand, and he leads us to the dance floor, and we dance the night away. When the ball drops at midnight, Amer kisses me, and I deepen the kiss as I pull him into me.

We all sing "Auld Lang Syne" and the party continues on.

"Take me to bed," I tell Amer.

"You don't have to tell me twice."

We say goodbye to everyone and make our way to the hotel. As I step out of my dress, I have to check it out. Amer was right. It looks good on the floor too. He lays me on the bed and kisses every inch of my body.

"Stellina, Happy New Year. This is our first of many, and I can't wait to experience them all with you."

I wrap my arms around his neck, I kiss him, I kiss him knowing that he's mine forever and I can't wait to spend forever with him.

Dear Readers,

I hope you all have enjoyed Christmas Delight. Amer and Mara-Lee are two of my favorite characters to write about. Of course, you'll be seeing them throughout the series and what's to come over time. I'm not done with Night's Bliss, not by a long shot. Next up in line is Halton's Pleasure. It should be released sometime in 2023. I haven't decided on a date just yet. But don't worry, I've got plenty more for you until then.

Sincerely,
E.C.

ALSO BY E.C. LAND

Devil's Riot MC

Horse's Bride

Thorn's Revenge

Twister's Survival

Reclaimed (Devil's Riot MC Boxset Bks 1 – 3)

Cleo's Rage

Connors' Devils

Hades Pain

Badger's Claim

Burner's Absolution

Redeemed (Devil's Riot MC Boxset Bks 4 – 6)

K-9's Fight

Revived Boxset (Devil's Riot MC Boxset Bks 7 — 9)

Red's Calm

Devil's Riot MC Originals

Stoney's Property

Owning Victoria

Blaze's Mark

Taming Coyote

Luna's Shadow

Choosing Nerd

Ranger's Fury

Carrying Blaze's Mark

Neo's Strength

Cane's Dominance

Venom's Prize

Devil's Ride (DRMC Boxset 1-5)

Protecting Blaze's Mark

Whip's Breath

Viper's Touch

Devil's Riot MC Southeast

Hammer's Pride

Malice's Soul

Axe's Devotion

Rebelling Rogue

Ruin Boxset 1-3

Remaining Gunner's

Devil's Riot MC Tennessee

Breaking Storm

Blow's Smoke

Inferno's Clutch MC

Chains' Trust

Breaker's Fuse

Ryder's Rush

Axel's Promise

Fated for Pitch Black

Tiny's Hope

Their Redemption Boxset 1 - 5

Fuse's Hold

Nora's Outrage

Tyres' Wraith

Brielle's Nightmare

Pipe's Burn

Their Salvation Boxset 6 - 10

Dark Lullabies

A Demon's Sorrow

A Demon's Bliss

A Demon's Harmony

A Demon's Soul

A Demon's Song

Dark Lullabies Boxset

Royal Bastards MC (Elizabeth City Charter)

Cyclone of Chaos

Spiral into Chaos

Aligned Hearts

Embraced

Entwined

Entangled

Ensnared

Crush Boxset 1-3

Entrapped

Night's Bliss

Finley's Adoration (Co-Write with Elizabeth Knox)

Cedric's Ecstasy

Arwen's Rapture

Satan's Keepers MC

Keeping Reaper

Forever Tombstone's

Hellhound's Sacrifice

Outrage Boxset 1 - 3

Toxic Warriors MC

Viking

Ice

War

De Luca Crime Family

Frozen Valentine (Prequel)

Frozen Kiss

Sons of Norhill Tops

Inheriting Trouble

Pins and Needles Series with Elizabeth Knox

Blood and Agony

Blood and Torment

Blood & Betrayal

Agony Boxset 1 - 3

DeLancy Crime Family with Elizabeth Knox

Degrade

Deprave

Detest

Desire Boxset 1 - 3

Deny

Demean

Raiders of Valhalla with Elizabeth Knox

Malicious

Sinister

Malevolent

Broken Boxset 1 - 3

Spiteful

Menacing

Deathstalkers MC with Elizabeth Knox

Kinetic

Available on Audible

Reclaimed

Cleo's Rage

Connors' Devils

Hades Pain

Badger's Claim

Faith's Tears

Life is never as easy as they make it out to be.

FAITH

Finding my way back to Axel, well, him finding me, it's been as if we're sailing on cloud nine. But what happens when another woman comes into the picture claiming she's Axel's and that they share a child together.

Do I believe her and her stories? Or do I trust in Axel? He claims it's all a lie, and he doesn't remember the woman. But tests don't lie, do they?

Our lives were torn apart for years, and now that we're finally happy and have our little family, this happens. My tears are all I have in the dark while I figure out what to do or where we go from here.

ASPEN

No one said life had a guidebook to help make it through times like now. One that led me to him. If they had, I would have taken a different path altogether. Instead, I struck a deal with him, giving him control over all that is me. Unfortunately, I didn't know my heart would be on the line, same as my next breath as danger came to his door.

NINES' TIME

(Back Matter)
Nines' Time

Innocence comes in several different ways, for her and for me.

NINES

Accused of something so vile, I've got to find a way to prove I'm not the one they're looking for. I didn't do it, and they know it. On top of that, she steps into my life, more like stumbles. Time stops with one look at her, and I see the vulnerability in her eyes.

I don't have it in me to go for what I want, not

when I've got this hanging over my head. But I can't let her go either.

She's mine for the taking. But will she believe me when it comes to the truth?

Facing Daemon

She's mine, only she refuses to face the truth.

DAEMON

I didn't see her coming. Not until it was too late. My life was good, and I had it all. My son means the world to me, and he has a good relationship with his mom. What I didn't need was the collision course of what crashes into me. She's been around the club. I know how she is and what she tastes like. What I don't know is why she's fighting me? I'll find the truth and make her face her demons by first facing me.

www.ingramcontent.com/pod-product-compliance
Lightning Source LLC
Chambersburg PA
CBHW020741160726
47993CB00006B/2557